I0744755

SUGAR COOKIES & ZOMBIE SECRETS: MYSTERY #1

(HARLYNN'S MYSTERY INVESTIGATIONS, #1)

JESSICA SORENSEN

Sugar Cookies & Zombie Secrets
Jessica Sorensen
All rights reserved.
Copyright © 2019 by Jessica Sorensen
This is a work of fiction. Any resemblance of characters to actual persons, living or dead, is purely coincidental. The author holds exclusive rights to this work. Unauthorized duplication is prohibited. No part of this book can be reproduced in any form or by electronic or mechanical means including information storage and retrieval systems, without the permission in writing from the author. The only exception is by a reviewer who may quote short excerpts in a review.
Any trademarks, service marks, product names or names featured are assumed to be the property of their respective owners, and are used only for reference. There is no implied endorsement if we use one of these terms.

ISBN: 9781939045485

For information: jessicasorensen.com
Cover design by MaeIDesign

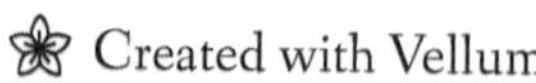
Created with Vellum

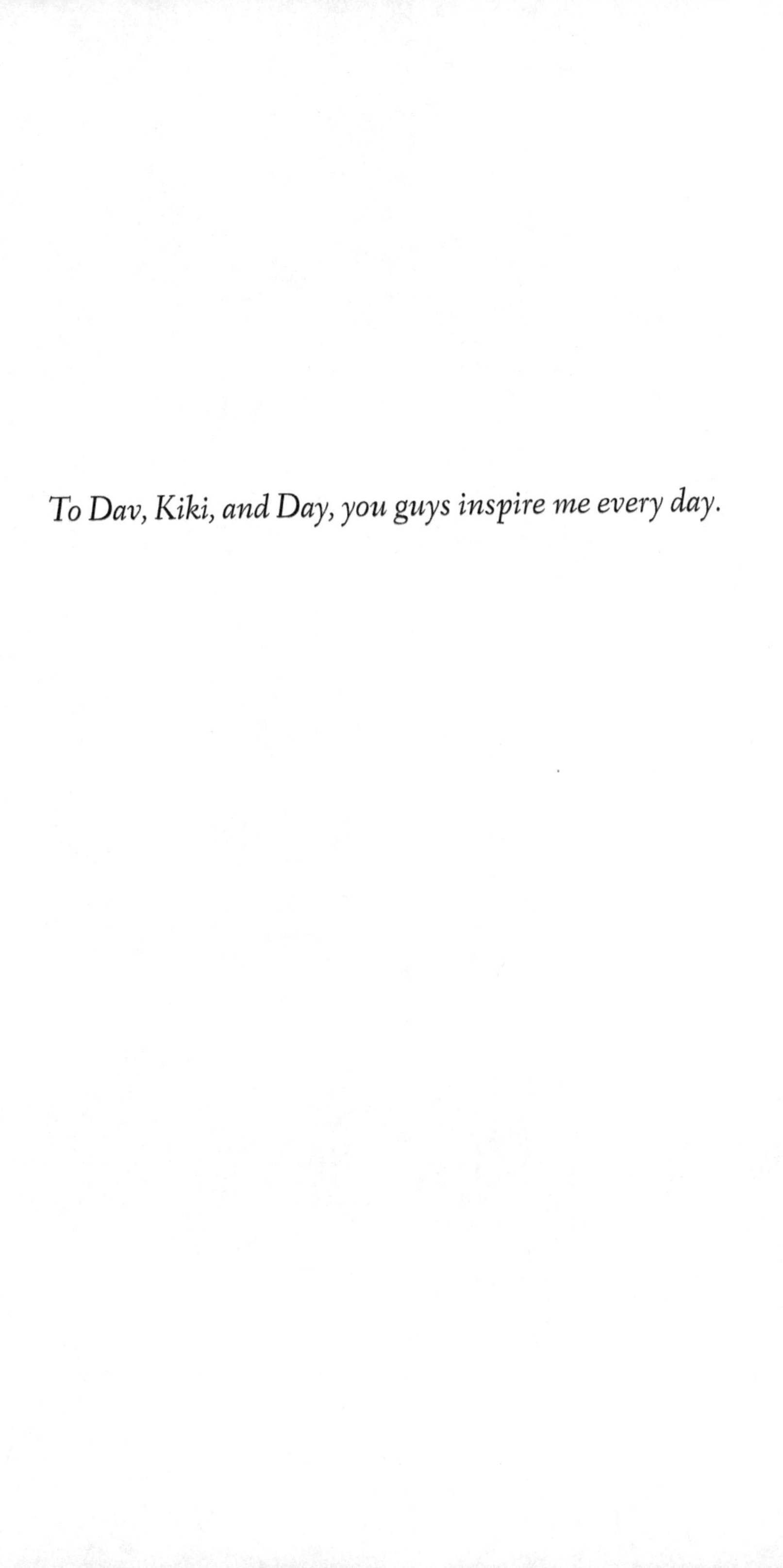

To Dav, Kiki, and Day, you guys inspire me every day.

I HAVE NO CLUE WHO I AM, IS THE FIRST THOUGHT I have when I open my eyes. When I glance around, however, that concern is quickly wiped out and replaced by, *Why the hell am I surrounded by zombies?*

Wait ... Did, like, the apocalypse happen and I slept through it or something?

I spring to my feet, worried that's exactly what happened, that a plague took over the world while I was asleep. That's when I get a better look at my surroundings and realize that something much stranger than the apocalypse has to be going on. Well, unless I somehow slept through an apocalypse next to a dumpster and beside a one-eyed cat that's currently staring at me.

Poor thing. It looks like it had a rough life. Is it even alive? Maybe it's a zombie cat ... Do zombie cats exist?

"Dude, are you gonna stand there all day or say something?" one of the zombies says in a surprisingly clear tone.

My gaze darts to her. She has tangled brown hair with several patches missing, which seems to be her theme since her skin is peeling off everywhere. Her clothes are worn and, like the cat, she only has one eye. With so much of her missing, I have no clue how old she is.

"Um ..." I stare at her stupidly, unsure how to react to her question. Unsure how to even react to this situation. I mean, in theory, it seems like I should be petrified but, weirdly, I just feel confused.

Zombie girl shakes her head then shuffles away from the rest of the zombies and closer to me. "Well, isn't this just awesome? Someone can finally see us and she's an idiot!"

"Hey, I'm not an idiot," I protest. "I'm just ..." I sweep my gaze across the other zombies, who are staring at me and drooling, and wonder if they're contemplating eating me. Then I wonder why they haven't yet. "Confused," I decide to finish with, shrugging.

Zombie girl rolls her one eye. "Obviously. I can see the stupid confusion written all over your face."

My confusion shifts to annoyance. "I'm not stupid. I just ... have no clue what's going on. I don't even know where I am." I glance around again, hoping something will click.

Nope.

I feel like a blank canvas that no one has started painting the story to yet. Or that the paint has been melted from it, just like the flesh of the zombie standing to my right.

Ew. I cringe as a glob of her skin melts from her body and splatters to the floor.

"You're in an alleyway with a bunch of zombies," zombie girl explains in an annoyed tone. "I don't know how that's not obvious"—she smirks—"other than if you're stupid."

My lips twitch, my annoyance spiking. Dude, zombie girl is a beotch. I don't say those words aloud, though, worried she might try to eat me or something.

"Look," I say as calmly as I can, "I have no idea what's going on. All I know is that I woke up here with a bunch of zombies. I have no idea why, where this is, or who I even am. So, if you could just tell me and clear up my stupid confusion, maybe I wouldn't be so annoying to you."

She lets out an exasperated sigh. "As much as I'd love to clear up your stupid confusion, none of us know anything about you, other than you're the only one in this world who can see and talk to us."

I blink at her, probably looking pretty damn stupid, but what she said ... "So, you're saying what? That I'm the only one in the world who can ... speak to zombies?"

She lifts a shoulder. "If that's what you want to call it."

My lips turn downward as reality sets in. "Why? And what the hell am I supposed to do with that? I mean, what's the point of speaking to zombies? Does it even have a point?"

She rolls her eye for the third time in a few minutes. "Of course it has a point. You can talk to the dead—you have a connection to the land of the dead and the living, which means you can find out secrets that everyone thought were taken to the grave."

A chill slithers down my spine. "That seems sort of like a dangerous gift ... Or, well, curse."

All she does is shrug again.

I open my mouth to ask her more questions, starting with how in the hell I ended up with this curse/gift, but the door to the building beside the dumpster is opened and an older woman with long, gray hair pulled up in a bun steps into the alley. She has on a T-shirt and jeans and is holding a broom, making my thoughts instantly go to, *Is she a witch?* That would seem like a ludicrous thought, except I am standing in an alley surrounded by a bunch of rotting zombies and a one-eyed zombie cat. Of course, the old woman doesn't seem to notice any of this, her gaze settling on me. Then her brows knit.

"What're you doing out here alone?"

I shrug. "I have no idea."

The crease between her brows deepens. "Did you get drunk and wander out here? I thought I locked the back door." Her puzzled look alters into suspicion. "Are you the asshole who's been jacking my booze from my storage room?"

I quickly shake my head, but then I pause. "Honestly, I don't know. I just woke up back here, and I ... I don't know who I am or how I got here." I know I sound crazy. Thankfully, though, her hard expression fills with sympathy.

"Come on, hon." She motions for me to follow her. "Let's go see if we can figure out what's going on."

Nodding, I hurry toward her as she steps back inside the building, more than ready to get the hell away from all these gawking, drooling zombies, and hoping I don't have to ever look at them again, because their rotting, oozing flesh is kind of disgusting to look at. Plus, seeing zombies seems like it should be weird. Then zombie girl offers me some ominous words as I'm passing her, squashing that hope.

"We'll see you soon, Harlynn," she whispers.

With that, they all disappear from the alley, which

should probably creep me out, except I'm more stuck on what she said.

Harlynn.

My name is Harlynn.

That knowledge should be a relief, but hearing it doesn't help me remember who I am. Also, why in the hell did zombie girl act like she didn't know me when she clearly does?

CHAPTER 2

THREE MONTHS LATER…

I'VE DECIDED I HATE BAKING. LIKE, UTTERLY DESPISE it. And yet, here I am, covered in flour, surrounded by bowls, sugar, measuring cups, and cooking sheets.

"Okay, maybe I was wrong about this one," Miss May, the older woman who found me in that alley three months ago, appears in the doorway.

I hold up my flour-covered hands. "I think so, too."

Pulling a face at the mess, she sets down the bag that she's holding and wanders over to the kitchen island, eyeing the mess in front of me. "I can't believe you can't bake. And sugar cookies of all things! That's one of the easiest things to bake."

Yeah, I beg to differ.

Honestly, when she suggested that I try baking this morning to see if I had some sort of hidden talent, I wasn't optimistic. I've been watching her bake and cook for three months, and I've never had the urge to dive in and help. But Miss May has been kind enough to let me live with her while I try to figure out who the hell I am, so I decided to give it a go. And now I feel like a failure, just like I have every other time she suggested I try something to see if I'm good at it. It's been her goal since she found me—figure out who I am and what makes me tick. So far, we haven't discovered much of anything.

All I really know about myself is that my name is Harlynn, and I'm probably around twenty-one years old, unless I'm one of those people who look older or younger than my age. I have long, wavy, brown hair, green eyes, a little bit of freckles on my nose, and I like to dress in dark clothing. Right now, I'm sporting a black shirt, shorts, a plaid overshirt, and unlaced black boots. I'm on the taller side and lean. I also know I can see zombies.

I haven't told anyone about my creepy gift/curse yet. And fortunately, for the sake of looking batshit crazy, the zombies have kept their distance ... for the most part. Zombie girl likes to randomly appear and convince me that I'm wasting my gift/curse, but she never specifies why. She's a vague one, that's for sure, and sometimes I wonder if she does it to drive me crazy.

"Here. Move out of the way so I can show you how it's done," Miss May says as she rolls up her sleeves.

I step to the side and reach for a towel to clean off my hands. "You want me to help you?" I ask, hoping she'll say no because, like I said, I'm not a huge fan of baking.

She eyes the bowl of bubbling batter. "Hmm ... Maybe you can just take the table and chairs down to the park and start setting up. I'm going to have to move quickly with this, or we'll be late for the event. Plus, I want these cookies to be perfect so I can sell the most cookies and rub it in Beth's weasel-like, overly made up face."

I bite back a smile. Beth, who I refer to as Miss Metherbee due to the fact that she hit me with her cane the first and only time I referred to her by her first name, is Miss May's rival for reasons she refuses to tell me. She's a mean, snarky old woman who believes in old-school traditions, like young people using respectful terms when directing the elderly. She also dresses like she thinks she's some 1920s starlet, only a starlet who can't color coordinate and who I'm fairly certain sometimes uses old curtains for clothing.

I nod in relief. "Yep, I can do that."

She shakes her head, an amused smile tugging at her lips. "By the sound of your eagerness, I take it that not only can you not bake, but you also hate doing it."

I chew on my bottom lip. "It's not that I hate it. It's just ..." I trail off as she gives me a stern look.

"What have I told you about sugarcoating shit?" She picks up the bowl of bubbling batter.

I sigh. "All right, I hate cooking."

"See? Was that so hard?"

"No."

"I can tell you're lying to me again, but I'm going to let it slide for now since we're so damn low on time."

She's not really upset. She's just a blunt person, something I discovered after moving in with her. Well, when I moved into the apartment above her garage. She was nice enough to set me up with a job at her bar, and she lets me drive around her extra car. She's probably the nicest person I've ever met. I mean, who just lets someone with no identity move in with them? For all anyone knows, I could be a serial killer or something. Though, I've never gotten the urge to kill anyone, but you get my point. No one knows who I am. Not even me. And that's scary, especially since I can talk to zombies, something I'm reminded of after I leave the kitchen, step outside, and find zombie girl standing in the driveway.

When I spot her, the temperature slightly drops, something that sometimes happens whenever a zombie is nearby.

"Still playing make-believe, huh?" she mocks as I step off the porch and head toward the garage to load up the table and chairs.

I ignore her, open the side door to the garage, and step inside.

Spiderwebs are everywhere, making me cringe. Yeah, that's another thing that I discovered about myself—I have a spider phobia. I was made aware of this the first time I found a spider crawling on me and screamed like a wild banshee. It wouldn't have been so embarrassing if I hadn't been at a brunch with Miss May, surrounded by a ton of townspeople who she had just introduced me to and told them of my story. So, not only was I the girl who couldn't remember anything about herself, but I also became the girl who knocked the punch all over the mayor because a spider was on my arm. A spider that crawled off before anyone else could see it. So, yeah, some people now look at me like I'm insane whenever we cross paths. And I guess, considering I have a one-eyed zombie trailing behind me right now, maybe they're on to something.

"You can't ignore us forever," zombie girl warns as I start sorting through the chairs while trying to avoid all the cobwebs. "One day, you're gonna realize that your gift can be useful."

I roll my eyes but don't say anything as I reach for a fold-up table.

"You know, if you keep this silent treatment up, maybe we won't even want to help you when the time comes," she spats.

When I still say nothing, she lets out a low and very zombie-like growl.

"Fine, but don't say I didn't warn you ... And FYI, you have a spider on your shoulder. Better start screaming and freaking out like you did at that brunch."

I squeal, darting my hand for my shoulder, but I can't see a spider on it.

When zombie girl lets out an evil laugh, I realize she's messing with me. I also realize how closely she's been watching me, since I didn't know she was at the brunch that day. That means she's been secretly stalking me.

Awesome. Zombies are stalking me.

I don't know what to do to with that, other than ignore the problem, something else that I'm apparently good at.

CHAPTER 3

Miss May owns two cars; an old, red Corvette and a 1969 dark blue Chevelle, which is what she lets me drive around. Both cars are gorgeous, and when I first climbed onto the leather seats that smell like a different era, the strangest sense of familiarity overwhelmed me.

It was day three after Miss May had discovered me. She used the car to drive me to the sheriff's office so we could talk to the sheriff on how to go about figuring out who I am. I was sitting in the passenger seat at the time, and as I ran my fingers over the leather seat, I could've sworn I'd sat on it before.

"Do you think that maybe I'm from this town?" I ask Miss May.

She shakes her head. "No, hon. I really don't."

I frown. "How can you be so sure?"

She sighs. "Because Hollows Grove is an extremely small town where everyone knows everyone else's business. There's not a single person here that I don't know. And when someone new moves in or we get a visitor, it's front page news, so ..." She shrugs and offers me an apologetic look. "I really don't believe you're from here."

"Then how did I end up here?" And why does being in this car feel so familiar?

She lifts her shoulder, a drop of worry flashing across her face.

I didn't understand the worry at the time. But after we talked to the sheriff, I was made aware of several different reasons as to why I could have such a huge case of amnesia, one being that I was faking it and that I was a criminal. But, after running my fingerprints and doing some research, the sheriff decided that probably wasn't the case. It also helped that, after seeing a doctor, we discovered that I'd recently suffered some head trauma, which explained the amnesia. Once that was discovered, a darker theory was established. That maybe someone had harmed me.

The problem is that I don't match any of the missing person cases in the country. Plus, my fingerprints don't appear in the system, and I don't exist online. It's like I literally appeared out of nowhere. Honestly, deep down, I wonder if perhaps that's a possibility. After all, I see freakin' zombies roaming around all the time! But I don't know … Everything about me seems human, so …

I tear myself away from my thoughts as I reach the park where the charity event is taking place. It's fairly crowded already, with booths lining the sidewalk, banners strung up everywhere, and a stage has been set up near the Hollows Grove cat memorial.

Yeah, so, apparently, Hollows Grove used to be overrun by stray cats. But, instead of freaking out about this, the townspeople embraced it. Then, one day, this big-ass storm blew through and wiped out like seventy percent of the cat population. So many people were upset that they decided to make a memorial for all the lost cats. They also hold this charity event every year to raise money for animal shelters, which I think is a really nice thing to do. I just find it weird they have a cat memorial. Then again, after living in this town for three months, I'm realizing that Hollows Grove is weird. So are a lot of the people who live here.

Speaking of weird …

"You made it." Miss Metherbee hobbles over as I'm climbing out of the car, her cane smacking the pavement. "I thought for sure you were gonna take off with Miss May's table and chairs."

I close the door with my back turned to her and roll my eyes. *Here we go.*

Miss Metherbee is convinced I'm a con artist who's playing Miss May so I can steal her stuff. I don't know why. Even if I were, Miss May isn't super wealthy. Sure, she has a nice house and she owns a bar, but I can't steal those things from her.

"Now, why would I do that?" I arch my brow at her as I round to the trunk where I stuffed the table and chairs. Since the trunk was too full to close, I had to secure it with a strap.

She shrugs, stopping beside me. "To sell them on the black market."

I undo the strap and open the trunk, resisting another eye roll. "I'm pretty sure that tables and chairs aren't hot black-market items."

She gives me a snide look. "You would know."

I have to bite my tongue and remind myself that she's a possibly slightly senile, old woman who might not even realize what she's saying.

"No, I don't." I grab a chair.

"Funny, you act like you know you don't, yet you supposedly don't remember anything about your old life." She smirks at me as she taps her heavily ringed fingers against the top of her cane.

Honestly, I don't even know how she can move her fingers with so many bulky rings on it. I swear, each one looks like it weighs three pounds or so. And her heavily decorated fingers are just the start of the overly excessive style that Miss Metherbee likes to wear.

Today, she has on a diamond necklace, ruby red shoes, a silk dress, and what looks like an antique curtain but I'm pretty sure is supposed to be a robe pulled over her shoulders. Her dyed hair is pulled into a high bun. If she was sporting a tiara, which I'm kind of surprised she isn't, I'd guess she was trying for a princess look. Although, I highly doubt that diamond necklace is real.

While Miss Metherbee likes to attempt to give off the appearance of wealth, she lives in a small apartment above her antique store that rarely has any customers.

As Miss Metherbee continues to smirk at me, I let out a sigh.

"Look, as much as I'd love to stand around here and convince you that I'm not some sort of black market expertise who's secretly working a con against Miss May so I can sell all her tables and chairs to make a whopping five bucks, I've got a booth to set up." Grabbing a chair from the trunk, I turn to head for the park. "It's been super fun talking to you, though." Sarcasm drips from my tone.

She narrows her eyes at me and parts her lips, but before she can get a word out, I quicken my pace. Still, I hear her mutter something about, "Stupid con artist," underneath her breath. I just keep on walking, ignoring my impulse to go back and talk shit with her.

Yep, another trait of mine that can either connect me to people or rub them the wrong way, something I quickly learned.

As I'm walking away, a sudden strange sense of coldness prickles up the back of my neck, like the kind whenever a zombie is around. I pause, glancing over my shoulder, expecting to see zombie girl. All that's there, though, is a glaring Miss Metherbee.

"So weird," I mutter before turning back around and continuing toward the park.

"Hey, Harlynn. I'm so glad you could make it," Stephanie, the woman hosting this event and who hosts pretty much every town event, greets me as I near the park entrance. She's all smiles and perfectly pressed pantsuit. Today, her suit matches the decorations of the event: pink and gold. It's a hideous combination, and I have no clue why she chose those colors for an event being held for animals. Truthfully, if I didn't know what the event was for, I'd just assume it was a tea party or a bridal shower or something.

I put on my best smile, knowing Stephanie is not the type of person I can use my snarky personality with. "Yeah, Miss May sent me down here to set up her table," I say, coming to a stop beside her, "after a very failed attempt at baking. And when I say failed, I mean *failed.*

Like, the batter looked straight out of a bubbling witch's potion type fail."

She immediately frowns. "Oh dear. I hope you're not planning on serving the cookies made from that batter."

"Well, we're not planning on serving them to everyone. Just the people that are on our bad side." I wink at her.

Her frown deepens. "Oh no, Harlynn. You can't sell bad cookies at my event. We need people to be happy and healthy so they'll make generous donations."

Well, I guess my joke fell flat.

"I was kidding," I explain to her.

"Oh." She lets out a forced laugh. "That was funny."

And that's my cue to leave.

"So, where should I set up?" I ask, shifting the chair I'm holding.

"Oh. Let me look it up." She taps on the iPad that she's holding and wavers her head from side to side as she looks at the screen. "Well, I marked a spot for Miss May over by the fountain, but maybe I should move her to by the swing set."

I mentally roll my eyes. The fountain area is considered a prime location at these events, while the swing set area, where all the kids hang out, doesn't get much traffic. And, since the table that raises the most money gets a ribbon, Miss May isn't going to be happy about losing her spot. My bet is Stephanie just wants to move Miss May due to the fact that she still thinks she's going to be serving bubbling potion cookies.

"Nah, the fountain area is fine," I insist.

She frowns. "Are you sure? Because I don't mind changing your spot. In fact, the swing set area could be the perfect place for your table and special cookies."

I shake my head. "Nah, we're good with the fountain. Besides, I heard moving areas right before an event is considered bad luck." I start to walk off before she can press the situation further.

"Harlynn," she calls out as I'm powerwalking away.

I almost keep walking, pretend to be deaf, but knowing Stephanie, she'd probably chase me down. So, sighing, I turn around and face her.

"What's up?"

She steps toward me. "Bad luck or not, I think I need to move you next to the swing set area. I just want to make sure everything runs smoothly and, from what you told me about the cookie situation at Miss May's ..." She pauses, offering me a sympathetic look. "I think it'd be best to let Miss Metherbee take the spot by the fountain, since her cakes look so delicious ... and un-bubbly." She offers me an exaggerated smile. "We wouldn't want to risk this event getting ruined by a bad case of group diarrhea."

Did she seriously just say the words group diarrhea?

I try not to snort a laugh, which becomes pretty easy when I realize the fuller picture of what she said.

Me and my smartass mouth.

Miss May is not going to be happy about losing her spot to her nemesis.

CHAPTER 4

AN HOUR LATER, I HAVE THE TABLE AND CHAIRS SET up and am sitting on a swing, waiting for this little shindig to start and for Miss May to arrive. Since it's getting close to starting time, I texted her, but she hasn't replied yet. I'm not too concerned. She has a knack for not answering her texts and for being fashionably late.

It's hot as hell out here, since it's mid-summer. The heat in Hollows Grove is humid, too, so I'm basically starting to sweat. As soon as Miss May shows up and I help her get all the cookies on the table, I plan on wandering over to the diner across the street to get some lunch and get out of this melting weather.

While this is the first summer that I can remember, I'm realizing I don't do well with extremely humid heat. I wonder what sort of climate I'm used to.

I always wonder what kind of person I was. If I wonder too much about it, though, it starts to bother me. But, what really bothers me is when my mind starts to overanalyze all the things that could've happened to me. Sometimes it takes a really dark path, down roads where I'm tied up and beaten, but none of those images feels real.

Nothing ever really feels real except for the present, which makes connecting to things and people complicated. The only person I've really been able to truly connect with is Miss May, but I even sometimes feel a disconnect with her.

I wonder if that'll ever change ...

As a shadow falls across me, I glance up and meet the blue eyes of Kingsley, the town sheriff. Although, he doesn't look like a sheriff, even when he's wearing the uniform. He's only twenty-two and is seriously the prettiest guy I've ever seen. Well, that I can remember seeing. I can't really picture the idea of anyone looking more gorgeous than him with his blond, chin-length hair and sky blue eyes framed with long, thick eyelashes. He's tall, lean, and right now, he's dressed in regular clothes—a pair of black jeans and a grey shirt.

When Miss May first took me to the sheriff's office and introduced me to him, I thought she was messing with me. I even snorted a laugh, which elicited a baffled look from Miss May and an amused, curious look from Kingsley. Seriously, though, he did not look like he could be a town sheriff. Turns out, he is, and a pretty good one.

He smiles down at me. "So, who did you piss off to get stuck in the swing set area?"

I grimace. "I didn't technically piss anyone off. I just made a joke to Stephanie about how I was baking for Miss May's table and my batter looked a little like a bubbly potion. But then I told her that Miss May had taken over the baking for me. She didn't believe me. And apparently, she was worried that the whole town was going to get a case of group diarrhea."

He cocks a brow. "Stephanie used the words *group diarrhea*? For reals?"

"Yeah, I thought it was weird, too. I seriously thought those types of words were like swear words to her. I guess I was wrong."

He shakes his head as he sits down on the swing beside me. "Nah. Stephanie's been friends with my mom for as long as I can remember, and I've never heard her use the word diarrhea. In fact, I once heard her use the term 'no-no words' after her son said crap. And he was sixteen years old at the time."

I snort a laugh. "Dude, I couldn't even imagine having a mother like that." I waver. "Well, I guess, technically, I could have a mother like that out in the world somewhere."

It grows silent then, and I worry I might've made things awkward, something that sometimes happens with people when I bring up my amnesia. Although, Kingsley usually isn't one of those people. When I glance at him, though, I realize that, once again, I've read someone wrong.

Damn, I'm really bad at that.

I wonder if I've always been that way.

"I'm actually glad you brought that up," he tells me, reaching into his pocket.

"You are?" I ask. "Because most people get all weird about it."

"Well, most people suck." He takes out a small envelope from his pocket and hands it to me.

"What's this?" I ask, taking the envelope from him.

"It's your new identification."

A drop of excitement rushes through me. Am I finally, *finally* going to have a full name? "But I thought you said it was going to take months to get this approved?"

He lifts a shoulder. "I had my dad make a few calls and get the approval pushed through quicker."

Kingsley's father is this retired, big shot lawyer who has connections everywhere, so I'm not surprised he was able to do this. What I am surprised about is that Kingsley would ask him for help. While he hasn't flat-out said it, every time anyone brings up his father, he gets this look on his face, like a mixture of hatred and disgust. Then again, I don't seem to be very good at reading people, so maybe I'm misinterpreting the look.

"Thanks for doing that." I smile then glance down at the envelope.

Suddenly, my excitement shifts to nervousness. Once I open this, I will have a full name. I will be this person. I will be accepting that I am this person. Does that mean I'm also accepting that I won't ever remember who I am?

I'm not sure.

"Where are your thoughts at, Har?" he asks with a hint of concern.

He's the only one in town who calls me Har, and I've always liked the sound of it. It makes me wonder if people used to call me that. So far, the nickname hasn't spread, like how Stephanie believes my diarrhea cookies are going to.

"It's nothing," I say with a dismissive shrug. "I was just thinking about what this means ... Having a full name ... Letting go of the idea that I'll ever figure out what my real name is. But I'm sure I'm making a bigger deal out of this than I need to."

He shakes his head. "It's completely understandable

that you'd want to know who you are. And this"—he taps the envelope—"doesn't mean you're letting go of the idea. It just means you get to have an identification and a name while we continue searching for your real name." He pauses, the corners of his lips quirking. "It also means that you can finally get your driver's license and I don't have to pretend anymore that I don't notice you driving around illegally all the time, even after I've told both you and Miss May that you need to stop doing that until you've taken your driver's test."

I feign dumb. "I have no idea what you're talking about."

He gives me a tolerant look. "So that wasn't you who pulled into the parking lot in Miss May's Chevelle? And I don't see you driving it every Friday and Saturday after your shift ends at that bar?"

As I spot Miss May striding across the grass with a stack of plates in her hands, I hurriedly jump to my feet. "Oh, look, there's Miss May." I dash toward her with his chuckle trailing after me.

"Hey," I start to greet her with a wave and a smile. But that smile fades as she reaches me and I see how pissed off she looks.

"Why in the shit is that damn psychopath, robe-wearing nutjob in our spot?" she snaps, her nostrils flaring.

"Well, funnily enough, it does have to do with shit," I try to crack a joke, but she only gets more worked up.

"As much as I like your shitty jokes, I want to know what happened," she demands.

Sighing, I steer her toward the table while I start explaining the disaster that has become today.

CHAPTER 5

AFTER I FINISH EXPLAINING TO MISS MAY HOW I lost our area, she immediately sets off to find Stephanie. In a way, I kind of feel sorry for her. While Miss May does have a soft side—the side that stepped in and helped me after she found me in the alley—she has a mean streak, too. And when that mean streak appears, watch out.

I once saw her throw a board game at her friend when she was losing. And she once tripped her best friend after she had told her that her cookies tasted like ass. Yeah, Miss May and her friends are a weird bunch. But that's okay. I like their weirdness and kind of fit in with it. At least, this new version of me does. Who the hell knows what the old, pre-amnesia me would've done?

Which reminds me. I haven't looked inside the envelope that Kingsley gave me.

I sit down in a chair behind Miss May's table, the space covered with plates full of delicious-looking, frosting cookies that are in the shapes of cats and dogs. They look so yummy, but Miss May warned me that, if I ate even a single one, she'd make me walk home. And since it looks like it's going to rain, I'm keeping my hands off them. But I'm so starving at this point that I'm debating whether or not it's worth the punishment to eat a few.

As I glance up at the clouds, I decide to distract my hands from cookies and tear open the envelope. Inside is a social security card and an identification card that lists the birthdate as exactly twenty-one years ago from the day I was found, which is the day we all decided should be my birthday. It was a tiring process to get all this stuff that required a lot of paperwork and meetings with a judge, but it would've taken a lot longer without Kingsley's help. Truthfully, a lot of people had no clue what to do with my case, so Kingsley ended up winging a lot of the process. Thankfully, it worked out.

"I need to do something nice for him," I mutter to myself as I examine my new ID card.

"Do something nice for who?" Miss May plops down in the chair beside me, looking worn out.

"Kingsley." I show her the ID card. "For helping me get this."

She puts on her glasses then leans over to examine the card. "Wow, that got here quicker than we all thought."

"I know," I agree, tucking the ID card back into the envelope with the social security card. "Kingsley told me he asked his dad for help in speeding up the process."

Amusement twinkles in her eyes as she leans back in the chair. "Did he now?" She faces forward in the chair as a woman approaches the table

"Um ... yeah." I eye her over. "Why did you look at me like that when you said that?"

"Looked at you like what?" She plays dumb but gives me the same look from out of the corner of her eye.

I narrow my eyes at her. "Don't play dumb with me. You know what look."

She arches a brow at me. "*I'm* the one playing dumb?"

My brows pull together. "What does that mean?"

She shrugs, looking back at the woman who's eyeing over the selection of cookies. "It means that you seem awfully oblivious to how that young man looks at you and how much he's always helping you. So, either you're just playing dumb or you're naïve. And by that dumbfounded look on your face, I'm going to go with the latter."

"Hey, I'm not naïve," I protest, speaking louder than I planned.

"Don't you dare scare away my customers, Harlynn," Miss May hisses from under her breath. "Because, while I may have been handed the shittiest area of this event, I'm still gonna sell the hell out of these cookies. And then, when I win that ribbon, I'm going to rub it all over Beth's face."

"Literally?" I joke.

She sneaks me a sly grin, letting me know that if she does win that ribbon, me and the rest of the town might get to witness a fight breaking out between two old ladies. I guess that's pretty much your typical Saturday in this town.

"Go get yourself some lunch so I can focus on winning that face-rubbing ribbon," Miss May says while shooing me away.

Sighing, I get to my feet and grab my wallet.

"And if you really want to thank Kingsley for his help," Miss May whispers under her breath before I walk off, "take him out on a date."

With that, she gives her full attention to her customer, leaving her final words swirling in my head.

She thinks Kingsley likes me? The most gorgeous guy I've ever seen?

I shake my head. No. There's no way. And even if there was, I couldn't take him out on a date. Not when I don't know anything about that part of my life. I mean, have I ever even dated? Had a boyfriend? Been in love? Kissed someone?

"Always so lost." Zombie girl appears by my side as I'm wandering across the grass, heading for the diner. "You know, maybe if you started listening to your gift more, you'd learn more about yourself."

"Yeah, like talking to the dead is going to get me anywhere," I mumble as I reach the street corner where a few people are waiting for the crosswalk sign to change. They all glance at me funnily then dash away when the sign changes.

Once they're out of earshot, I say to zombie girl, "Other than looking crazy."

"Maybe crazy is your thing," she suggests, shuffling beside me as I start to cross the street.

"Maybe," I agree. "But that doesn't mean I need to embrace the crazy right now." I quicken my pace, leaving her behind.

"Eventually, you will," she calls after me. "You'll see ..."

Her words fade as I rush into the diner, but worry still stirs through me.

It's like she's trying to warn me of something. Something that has to do with my gift/curse of being able to talk to the dead, which can't be a good thing.

CHAPTER 6

THE DINER IS PRETTY EMPTY DUE TO MOST OF THE
town getting their food at the event, which is fine, since
crowded places sometimes make me feel claustrophobic.

Deciding I need some private space to calm down and
collect myself, I put in my order at the register then plop
down in a corner booth. My food gets brought out quickly
—thank God—and I dive in, stuffing my face with a
hamburger and a buttload of fries.

I eat in silence, my mind crammed with thoughts of
why I can see the dead and what that curse could possibly
do for me. Because, so far, it's done nothing but give me a
headache and make me realize what the stench of rotting
flesh smells like.

As I'm sitting there, picking at the last of my fries and
staring out the window, watching people walk by, a bolt

of lightning suddenly snaps across the cloudy sky. Moments later, thunder booms. And that's when the rain starts pouring from the sky. Only about a minute after that, it's coming down so hard that the streets start to flood.

I frown, watching the puddles take over the sidewalk. "Dude, Miss May is going to be so pissed off if that event is canceled and she doesn't get that ribbon to wipe all over Beth's face." Then again, I wouldn't put it past her to find something else to wipe in Beth's face.

"I think that's the least of Miss May's problems." Zombie girl materializes beside my table, strangely looking wet, like she's been standing outside in the rain.

I drop the fry I was holding as the stench of her reaches me. "What does that mean?"

She gives a pressing glance toward the entrance door. "Go have a look for yourself."

Beyond confused and worried, I jump to my feet and rush outside into the rain, jogging for the park where a crowd has started to build, despite the crappy weather.

At first, I think everyone is just being super supportive of the cause. Then I see the flashing lights and Miss May being guided into the back of a police car by a uniformed deputy.

"What the hell?" I mutter, pushing through the crowd, trying to get to her as rain pours down on me. But before I can reach her, the deputy has her in the back seat of the patrol vehicle and shuts the door.

"Shit."

The rain already slowing to a drizzle, I scan the crowd, searching for Kingsley. He may not be on duty, but he can at least give me a good idea of what's going on. He's the only one I really trust to give me info without a bunch of gossip being put in with it.

Finally, I spot him standing near the restrooms, talking to another deputy with his arms crossed. I push people out of my way as I hurry toward him, highly aware that almost everyone has turned to gawk at me, but I disregard their looks as I approach Kingsley.

When his gaze finds mine, so does the deputy's that he's chatting with. His name is Ben, and he's probably around my alleged age. He actually lives next-door to Miss May and spends a lot of time either perving on the neighbors behind him or watching the birds in a large tree near the house. I'm still a little unsure about which one.

Ben strides toward me. "Ma'am, step back." He sticks his hand out and urges me to back up.

I roll my eyes. "Don't *ma'am* me, Benjamin. You know my name, just like I know how you like to spend your Saturday afternoons." The sassy words just sort of leave me without any forethought, and both Ben and I pause.

"Um ..." Ben scratches the back of his neck and shifts

his weight. "I don't ... Um ... What?" He's at a loss for words, either because of my snark or because he really is perving on the neighbors.

"It's okay, Ben. I've got this." Kingsley walks over to me, gently putting his hand on my arm and steering me away from Ben and the restrooms.

"Where are we going?" I mumble, again aware of how many people are gawking at me. "And what the hell is going on? Why was Miss May arrested? And why the hell is everyone staring at me like I've sprouted a unicorn horn out of my head?"

"Just a second," he mutters, his gaze sweeping the playground and grass area. Then, with his hand still on my arm, he steers us out of the park, across the street, and into an alley nestled between the diner and an herbal store.

"What's with the secrecy?" I ask in a quiet tone as he removes his hand from my arm.

He lets out a loud exhale and rakes his fingers through his hair, his worried gaze settling on mine. He looks very uneasy, which makes me extremely uneasy. But nothing could prepare me for what he's about to say.

"It's Miss May," he says. "She's been arrested for murder."

CHAPTER 7

At first, I think I'm hallucinating. I mean, I do see zombies everywhere, so ...

I blink at him confusedly. "Huh?"

He releases another audible sigh, dropping his hand to his side. "You know Mr. Douglas, the owner of the shop next to Beth Metherbee's store?" he asks, and I nod. "Well, he was found dead in the restroom and someone pointed a finger at Miss May; says they saw her do it."

My jaw nearly smacks the asphalt. "Well, they're lying. Miss May would never, ever hurt someone."

"I know that," he agrees. "For now, though, we had to arrest her."

Irritation simmers underneath my skin. "Why, if you know she didn't do it?" I shake my head as annoyance swells through me. "And who the hell said Miss May did it?"

He offers me an apologetic look. "You know I can't give out that information."

"Like this whole town isn't gossiping about it already. If I want to find out, I can just walk over to the park and ask someone ..." I chew on my bottom lip. "Although, I noticed a lot of people staring at me. What was that about? Because Miss May was arrested?"

Wariness floods his features. "Let's not worry about that right now." He takes a step toward the exit of the alley. "I need to get down to the sheriff's office and see if there's any way we can get bail posted for Miss May. With how severe the crime is ... it might be complicated."

I follow him as he leaves the alley. "Please tell me you'll be able to get her out on bail." The idea of Miss May, the woman who took me in when I had no one, sitting in some dirty jail cell is making my stomach churn.

He reaches over and gives my hand a squeeze. "I'll do my best. I swear I will." When I continue to frown, he stresses, "Har, I care about Miss May as much as you do ... She's helped me out a lot ..." He swallows hard. "Even when no one else would."

Questions burn at the tip of my tongue. I knew Kingsley and Miss May knew each other, but I thought it was like how everyone in this town knows everyone.

Clearly, they know each other better than I thought. But how? And what did Miss May do for Kingsley?

I could just ask him. Maybe I would have if we hadn't reached the park and the chattering of the town gossip reached my ears.

Suddenly, I realize why everyone was—and still is—staring at me. And why Kingsley was so hesitant to tell me.

Apparently, everyone believes that I'm somehow involved in Douglas's murder.

CHAPTER 8

I'VE ALWAYS KNOWN THAT SOME OF THE townspeople don't like me, that they believe I am an outsider and therefore trouble. I just wasn't aware how much they hated me.

I am now, though.

"Murderer," Mable, the woman who owns the grocery store, hisses at me as I walk past her. "You did this. I know you did. And then you framed Miss May."

I do my best to tune her out and continue making my way through the crowd, keeping close to Kingsley.

"You should be burned at the stake," Frank, the mailman, sneers at me as I pass him. Then the little, old twerp throws a stick at me, pegging me in the eye.

"Hey," I growl at him, covering my stinging eye with my hand. "That freakin' hurt, Frank."

"Good. I hope you hurt," he snaps, stepping toward me, "for what you did to Mr. Douglas." Then he starts to reach for me to do who knows what.

Suddenly, this strange urge to lift my arm and clock him in the face rises through me. My fingers start to curl inward, and I lift my fist, fully planning on giving in to the urge. But before I can, Kingsley moves between Frank and me.

He faces Frank and places his hand against Frank's chest. "If you try to hurt Harlynn, Frank, then I'll have to arrest you. And if I do, then we're going to have to finally address all your unpaid tickets that I've been pretending you don't have."

Frank narrows his eyes, but he steps back. "Whatever. I don't know why they let a little punk like you run this town. Things were so much better when Jerry was in charge."

"Jerry was fired for tampering with evidence and stalking," Kingsley reminds him. "So I think you know that's not true."

"Whatever," Frank grumbles then tosses one final look of hatred in my direction before stomping off.

Kingsley immediately turns toward me, his gaze zeroing in on my eye. "Are you okay?"

I nod, blinking a few times until my eye stops watering. "Yeah. I just didn't realize Frank hated me so much."

"He doesn't hate you," he assures me. "This town just gets caught up in drama sometimes and likes to point fingers at the easiest targets."

I crinkle my nose. "You think I'm the easiest target?"

"I think everyone *thinks* you are." He gently brushes his fingers across my clenched fist, reminding me of how I was about to punch Frank. "I don't know, though. I'm thinking with how fast you made that fist, you're definitely not."

I wrestle back a frown. "You saw that, huh?"

He nods, his lips tugging into a half-smile. "It's okay. It's good to have protective instincts. And Frank was coming at you to do who knows what. That man can be questionable sometimes."

Maybe he's right. Still, I can't get over how fast I reacted, like I'd been in a fight before.

"It was instinctive," I mutter, unclenching my fist and flexing my fingers. "I mean, the urge to hit him."

He searches my eyes with a guarded expression. "Does that sort of stuff happen a lot? I mean, do you feel instincts?"

I shake my head. "No, not usually. Honestly, not much has happened since ... well, since I woke up in that alley with no memory of who I am."

In fact, I've spent most of the last three months living an ordinary, structured life that consists of going to work, grocery shopping, cleaning the house, attending town events, and helping Miss May. This is the first real event that's steered off the path of mundane. Not that I'm glad Miss May is being accused of murder.

"I should probably get down to the sheriff's office," I announce, "and check on Miss May."

Kingsley nods, staring at me for a beat longer. "Yeah ... So should I." He steps back from me. "I'll meet you there, okay? I'm just going to talk to Ben and get some more details before I head down."

I nod, and then we part ways, him heading toward the restrooms while I start to make my way through the crowd toward the parking lot, doing my best to ignore all the rude comments being thrown in my direction. That urge to curl my fingers inward lingers underneath my flesh, leaving me to wonder why.

Why am I suddenly feeling urges when I've felt nothing but confusion for the last handful of months? It's almost like I've been drifting in a confused haze and that haze is now beginning to lift. But again, why?

Better yet, who framed Miss May? Because I know someone had to. Miss May, while feisty, isn't a killer. I know that for a fact.

"Man, if only there was someone you knew who could give you all the details of what happened." Zombie girl materializes by my side, her rotting flesh shedding, her grey lips twisted into a smirk.

"Do you know what happened?" I whisper once we're out of earshot of the gossiping crowd.

She shrugs. "Maybe."

"I doubt you do." No, I'm guessing she's just baiting me to talk to her, like she usually does.

Deciding I've had enough of her coded conversations, I quicken my pace. Surprisingly, she lingers back.

I expect her to leave like she typically does after dropping one of her riddled statements on me, but then she calls out, "I know who accused Miss May. Just like I know who actually killed the shop owner."

I freeze, a chill slithering up my spine as I slowly turn around to face her. My lips remain sealed as I eye her over, attempting to figure out if she's lying or not. Weirdly, her expression is neutral. Not even her smirk is visible.

"Is that the truth?" I question, inching toward her. "Because you've never said anything like this before. In fact, when I asked you what happened to me, you said you didn't know."

"And I don't know," she tells me. "But you never really died. Douglas, however, did. And he's the first person to die in this town since you arrived here, so of course I haven't said anything like this before."

I sneak a glance around, noting people are staring at

me from the distance. "Okay ..." Not wanting to look crazy, I whisper, "Can we talk about this in the car?"

"You care what people think?" she questions with an arch of her brow.

"Um ... When they're threatening to burn me at the stake, I do. Not that I actually believe anyone will, but ... still."

"You shouldn't believe that," she warns, wisps of her dark, thin hair blowing into her face as the wind kicks up.

Lightning illuminates the sky and thunder booms. Apparently, the storm isn't over yet.

"Why not?" I ask, my gaze bouncing from the darkening sky to her.

She lifts a shoulder. "Because some people in this town aren't trustworthy."

I flick a glance back at the restrooms, thinking about what just occurred. "Yeah, I'm starting to see that." I bite on my bottom lip, my gaze returning to her. "Look, I know you and I don't get along very well, but I need to know what happened. So, can we please go talk about this more in my car?"

Instead of answering me, she poofs into thin air.

Lovely.

Damn zombies are really starting to get on my nerves. And it doesn't help my irritation when another bolt of lightning flashes across the sky and the rain begins drizzling down on me.

Sighing, I spin around and jog toward my car, fully planning on driving straight to the sheriff's office. But, when I slide into the driver's seat, I find zombie girl sitting in the passenger seat with a bored look on her face.

She gives an exaggerated yawn. "Took you long enough."

"Yeah, well, some of us can't just materialize wherever we want."

"Yeah, I know. I'm awesome." Right as she says it, she picks a long flake of skin off her oozing arm.

"Yeah ... I wouldn't use the word awesome, but I guess being able to spontaneously materialize does have some perks." I bite back a gag as she flicks the skin onto the floor.

As I rev the engine, she leans back in the seat, getting comfortable, then reaches forward to mess around with the stereo.

"So ... are you gonna tell me who's trying to frame Miss May?" I finally ask. "Or just sit there and pick at your skin?"

Smirking at me, she peels off another layer and drops it onto the car floor.

I bite my tongue, knowing she's baiting me. Who knows for what reason?

After staring at me for an oozing beat, she finally rolls her eye. "Whatever. I like you better when you complain." Her gaze lands on the windshield covered in raindrops, and she stares outside, lost in thought.

"You know, I didn't want to be this," she states in an emotionless tone. "I always believed that when you died, you just died, you know? Never did I think I'd become this rotting version of myself who has to spend her time trying to convince some dense woman to use her gift."

I feel sorry for her in that moment, enough that I allow the dense comment to slide.

"I'm sorry you have to be a zombie. But, as for me using my gift ... up until now, I haven't really seen the point of it. And honestly, I'm still kind of questioning the purpose."

She elevates a brow. "You can see the dead, Harlynn, which means you have a connection to the living and the dead."

I grip the wheel, watching raindrops splatter against the windshield. "You've said that before, but you've never explained what the point of having this ability is."

She blows out an exasperated sigh. "Come on; let's go."

"Where?"

"To show you what the purpose of your gift is."

Confusion tap dances through me. "Where are we going?"

She reaches to put on her seatbelt ... which ... What?

"To Beth Metherbee's store," she says as she fastens the seatbelt.

My brows knit. "Why?"

She reclines back in the seat. "Because she's the one who told the police that Miss May killed Douglas."

CHAPTER 9

Maybe I should've guessed it on my own. With how much Miss May and Miss Metherbee fight, it does make sense.

But, does it? Does some ancient feud between two old women lead to one of them falsely accusing the other of murder?

I shake my head. "No. There's no way. I mean, I know they hate each other, but ..." I trail off when zombie girl raises her brows. "What?"

"Really?" She stares at me like I'm an idiot. "Hatred makes people do stupid things all the time."

She has very valid point, but ... "I just don't see Miss Metherbee being that cruel," I explain. "I mean, yeah, she's kind of bitchy and vile, and she hates Miss May, but ... that doesn't mean she'd falsely accuse Miss May of murder."

Zombie girl continues to stare at me like I'm a moron. "All right then. Let's go find out."

I scratch my arm. "What're we going to do?"

"Break into her house."

"And how is that going to help me get Miss May out of jail?"

She rolls her eye. "Look, I'm trying to help you. But I can't if you won't let me."

I shake my head. "Why can't we just ask Douglas who killed him? I mean, if I can talk to the dead and he's dead ... Shouldn't he be lurking around somewhere?" I glance out the window, my gaze skimming the park.

"Douglas isn't part of the dead yet," she utters. "And if we can solve his death quickly enough, then he won't ever have to be."

I turn my head to look at her. "Are you saying that all these dead zombies I've been seeing exist because their deaths haven't been solved?" When she nods, acting strangely quiet, I add, "Is it ... bad? Being one of you?"

Once again, she looks at me like I'm the dumbest person alive before she snaps, "Look at me, Harlynn! My skin is rotting off, puss is leaking out of my skin, my hair is falling out, and I smell like roadkill made a baby with spoiled eggs. Plus, as an added bonus, I have to deal with your dumb ass. Does that seem like something that would be pleasant?"

Feeling like a dumbass, I mutter, "No."

"Okay then." She turns her head toward the window. "So, now you know what's at risk if you don't use your ability." She leaves it at that, but I have so many questions, ones I doubt she'll answer.

I reach for the shifter, put the car in reverse, back up, and steer onto the road, driving toward Miss Metherbee's and crossing my fingers that I'll be able to prove Miss May's innocence.

If what zombie girl is saying is true, that figuring out who the hell killed Douglas so maybe he won't end up a walking, molting, oozing corpse, then that haunts me.

CHAPTER 10

"So this is where Beth lives?" Zombie girl muses as she stares at the dingy, brick building in front of us.

I parked out back to avoid risking being seen. With so many people in town believing I played a part in Douglas's death, I thought it was a good idea that no one sees me snooping around in Miss May's accuser's place. Although, I'm unsure how I'm going to even snoop around when Miss Metherbee's store is closed due to, as the sign on the back entrance door states, "*A lavish event full of glitz and glam that only the most important people have been invited to attend.*"

"I wonder if she actually believes that shit," zombie girl remarks as she eyeballs the sign.

"Have you seen how she dresses and acts? Of course she believes that shit."

Zombie girl chuckles. "You know, I think I might like this side of you."

I tilt my head to the side in confusion. "What side?"

She gives a half-shrug. "This snarky, sarcastic side that rarely comes out yet has made a pretty big appearance today."

I arch a brow. "Yeah, I have been feeling pretty weird today. What's up with that?"

She shrugs again.

I internally sigh. "Dude, what's up with you and shrugging? I'm starting to wonder if the move is like some weird zombie muscle twitch or something."

She bites back an amused grin. "Does it annoy you?"

I nod. "Yeah."

"Good. Then I'm gonna keep doing it." With that, she walks forward, dragging one of her feet across the ground.

I hurry after her. "Where are you going, zombie girl?"

"Inside. Obviously." She rolls her one eye. "You know, you call me zombie girl all the time and whatever—it's a fitting name, so I let it slide—but I'm seriously considering calling you stupid girl." She stops in front of the door. "I mean, it only seems fair if we're gonna give each other fitting nicknames."

I stop beside her and roll my eyes. "You're kind of a bitch."

"Yeah, I know. Maybe you should start calling me bitch girl."

"Nah, zombie girl is way more fitting."

"Really?" she asks dubiously.

I throw a pressing glance at a rotting section of her arm that has a bubble of blood on it. Right at that moment, it pops, spraying droplets of blood and puss all over the rest of her arm.

Her lips twitch in annoyance. "I may look like a zombie, but I'm way more of a bitch. Trust me."

"You really hate being a zombie, don't you?"

"I'm not even going to answer that stupid question."

"Good, because it was kind of rhetorical."

Surprise flickers in her eyes, and then a sly smile spreads across her face. "And there's that snarky attitude again."

I replay my words, highly aware she's correct, but I have no idea what that means, other than I evidently have a talent for being snarky. Again, I question why this trait is surfacing so potently now of all times. Unless ..."Am I starting to subconsciously remember who I am?" I ask aloud.

"I'm not sure," she replies then reaches for the door. "But, how about we find out what other secret talents you've got hidden inside that stupid head of yours?" With that, she pulls open the door.

For a flash of a second, the thought crosses my mind that maybe the store is open since the door is unlocked, but then I hear an alarm siren off from inside.

"Shit." Panicking, I start to back away, preparing to bolt, but she skitters behind me to push me forward, which looks really weird since only one of her legs is currently working properly. And yet, she manages to move as swiftly as a ... well, as an asshole zombie who's pushing someone into a building with an alarm going off.

Caught off guard by her abrupt ability to move so quickly, I end up tripping over my feet and falling into the store, landing on the floor on my hands and knees.

I hastily leap to my feet and whirl around to run back outside, but she scurries into the store and slams the door shut, barricading us in.

"Move," I warn, clenching my fist. "Or I'm gonna make you."

"What're you gonna do?" she questions amusedly. "Kill me? Newsflash: zombies are already dead. Or did the rotting, decaying flesh not give that away?"

"No, it did ..." I huff out a breath, trying to remain calm. "Look, please just let me out before the cops show up."

"The cops won't show up if you disable the alarm before they're notified."

"Awesome plan, except I don't know how to disable an alarm!" My tone oozes sarcasm.

She cocks a brow. "You sure about that?"

I open my mouth to say *yes*, but then seal my lips back shut. *Am I sure about that?*

No, I'm not really sure about anything.

I twist toward the wall where the code box to the alarm is located, my fingers twitching ever so slightly, which is so freakin' odd. Then I edgily make my way over there and reach for the box, uncertain of what to do. Well, I think so anyway, though it's like my fingers have a mind of their own as they open the cover to the code box.

Beneath it are buttons to enter a code, but that's not what I need. No, what I need is to get underneath the button section. How I know that, I have absolutely no idea. Just like I have no damn clue why I reach up, pluck a hairpin from my hair, and unscrew the lid to the button section. Then I tug on a wire and ... just like that, the alarm goes silent.

"Took you long enough. You're lucky it's not a very high-tech alarm," zombie girl remarks, shuffling up beside me.

"It's also really old," I say, my words confusing me. "Although, I have no fucking clue how I know that."

Her lips tug upward into a semi-amused, rotting smile.

"You know, that's one of the first times I've heard you say fuck."

Now that she's pointed it out, I become aware she's right.

Just who the hell am I? A woman who knows how to disable alarms? Who swears so casually? Who sees zombies? Though, I'm unsure if the latter was something I could do before the memory loss. My guess is probably not.

"So, now what do I do?" I ask as I stick the hairpin back into my hair.

She leans against the wall, looking as bored as can be. "What do your instincts tell you to do?"

I lift a shoulder, twisting toward the doorway that leads to the store section of the building. "I'm not sure ..." I trail off as that sense of coldness that I sometimes feel when I'm around the dead and, for some weird reason, when I was near Miss Metherbee earlier today flows over me.

"Where's that coming from?" I move farther into the room, tracking the coldness across the store and to a stairway that leads to what I'm guessing is the section of the building where Miss Metherbee lives. I chew on my bottom lip with my hand on the banister as I stare up into the darkness.

"Afraid of the dark?" zombie girl mocks from just

behind me.

I shake my head. "No." But the truth is that I am. I'm afraid of going back to that darkness that I felt right before I woke up in that alley.

While I really don't want to go up there, the urge to follow the coldness is too powerful to disregard, so I start up the stairs, each step creaking underneath my weight and making me cringe.

It feels like an eternity passes before I reach the top, but I finally get there. Then, instead of turning on the lights, I dig my phone out and flip on the flashlight.

"Look that that," zombie girl comments from behind me. "Your instincts kicked in again."

"You act like I used to do this kind of stuff in the past?" I scan the light around the room, along the sofa, the unmade bed in the corner, the cluttered desk stacked with papers, the empty paint cans all over the floor ...

What the shit? Empty paint cans?

"Did she recently redecorate?" I ask as I step farther into the room.

"Do you smell fresh paint?"

"No."

"Well, then I guess you have your answer."

"It's not really an answer, though." I stop beside one of the empty paint cans, crouch down, and look inside it. "Red ..." I glance at the label. "Blood red to be exact." I crinkle my nose. "I didn't realize they made paint that matched the color of blood."

"They make a paint color for every sort of shade these days," zombie girl remarks. "They even make one that matches the puss leaking out of my flesh."

I pull a face. "Who would wanna paint that color on anything? No offense."

She shrugs. "None taken. I know my puss bubbles are hideous."

I make no remark, too distracted by the bad vibe I'm getting. "Something's off in this room, but I can't figure out what."

"You should probably look around," zombie girl says, "because crouching down isn't gonna get you anywhere. Well, except for a bladder infection."

I throw her a befuddled look. "You can't get bladder infections from squatting."

"Really?" she muses. "Huh. I thought that was a human thing. Maybe I'm thinking of demons."

I blink at her. "What?"

"What, what?" Her eye sparkles with amusement.

Um ... "You just said demons exist."

"No, I said I think it's demons that can get bladder infections from squatting too long."

"I can't ..." I shake my head, pushing to my feet. "Demons exist?"

She rolls her eye. "Yeah, so? Zombies exist, too. Obviously. But I'm not sure why you're making a big deal about this."

"I'm just a little confused ..." I press my lips together, unsure how to react. "It's just weird thinking demons exist."

"Yeah, well, to avoid having this same conversation several times, I should also probably tell you that witches, werewolves, faeries, vampires, and pretty much every other mythical creature exist as well."

"I ... I'm not sure how to reply to that."

"You don't need to reply to anything, since I wasn't really asking a question."

She may not have been, but a ton burn on the tip of my tongue. She must sense the incoming questions, too, because she says, "Look, we don't have time for your stupid questions right now. But later, when you've solved this case, we can sit down and I'll answer the dumb questions that I can tell you want to ask right now. Well, the ones that I can."

"Okay." I chew on my bottom lip. "Can I just ask you one?"

She blows out a dramatic sigh. "If you must."

"Does ...? I mean ..." *Just spit the words out, Harlynn.* "Do other people know this sort of stuff exists?"

"Some do," she answers, observing me closely. "But I have a feeling you're referring to specific people."

"I am actually." I scratch my neck. "Like Miss May, Kingsley, and ... Well, that's really all the people I want to know about at the moment."

She smirks. "Now, what would be the fun in telling you that?"

"Because then I wouldn't have to be confused and annoy you," I suggest with an innocent shrug.

She considers my request with a wicked glint in her eye that makes me want to throat punch her. Well, maybe not since puss is currently leaking from a hole in her esophagus.

"I'll tell you what," she says. "Find the clue here, and I'll give you that answer."

"Whatever." Frustration bubbles through me as I glance around the room. "I know you're doing this just to mess with me."

When she just smiles, I grit my teeth and start searching for clues, wondering why this is so important to her. Why do I need to solve this case? What does she know?

Whatever it is, I'm sure she won't share it with me, so I focus on finding ... well, something. Honestly, I'm not positive what I'm looking for, but I make my way over to the desk and glance through the pile of papers—or receipts, as I find out.

I stumble on a receipt for a purchase made by Douglas a handful of days ago. The purchase price was for just a little over ... "Ten thousand fucking dollars?" And there's my sailor's mouth making a grand appearance again. Seriously, though ... "What the hell would you buy in this kind of a store that was worth that much? And better yet, how did Douglas end up with that much money? Not that it's impossible, but still ..."

I flip the receipt over to see what the purchase was for, but it's been blacked out with a marker. However, there's also a strange marking on the back, a hand drawing of some sort of circular symbol with smaller symbols bordering it, almost like a code.

"What is this?" I mutter as I lift the receipt up in front of me and shine the light directly on it to see if I can make out anything underneath the blacked out section. Nope. Someone dragged the marker pretty damn thoroughly across the paper.

I lower the receipt with my brows knit. "Why would Miss Metherbee black out the purchase?" Well, unless she didn't want anyone to see what Douglas had bought from her. But again, why? "And what the hell is this weird symbol?" And why not just destroy the receipt instead of blacking out the item? Unless she needs it for tax purposes. Still, doesn't the item need to be listed on the receipt for that?

Apparently, even back before I lost my memories, I wasn't an expert on taxes, because not a single idea comes to me. Truthfully, none of this came to me on my own. I only came here because zombie girl told me to. And I only found the receipt because the coldness that constantly plagues me led me up here.

I should just set the receipt down and walk away. It's not like I know what I'm doing. I'm not a detective. I don't need to get involved in this. And yet, I find myself taking a picture of the receipt, along with the strange symbol on the back, before putting it back into the pile. Then I turn around and let my gaze scan the room again, seeing if that cold vibe will lead me to another clue ... Well, if that's even what you can call the receipt.

After about a minute ticks by and the room temperature rises instead of plummets, I decide it's time to leave. Plus, zombie girl has ditched me, which pisses me off.

She said she'd tell me who knows about paranormal creatures if I found the clue. Now I found the damn clue, so ..."You owe me a secret," I mutter before heading out.

On my way down the stairs, my phone rings from inside my pocket. I dig it out and see Kingsley's name flash across the screen.

I almost don't answer it, since I'm currently in the

process of committing a crime, but then I worry that he might be calling with an update on Miss May, so I tap *answer* and put the phone up to my ear.

"Hey." Weirdly, I sound as calm as can be, making me again question who the hell I was before this life.

A criminal?

"Hey," he replies, and I can hear chatter and phones ringing in the background. "I just got to the sheriff's office ... Are you here? I didn't see you anywhere and everyone is telling me you haven't gotten here yet."

Shit. Through zombie girl leading me on this little murder solving scavenger hunt, I'd totally forgotten that I told Kingsley I'd meet him at the sheriff's office.

"Um ... no, I haven't gotten there yet." I quicken my pace, reaching the bottom of the stairway and hurrying toward the back door. "I had to stop to get gas and the lines to the pumps were really long. I'll be there soon, though." I stop in front of the alarm box and, like some sort of badass alarm fixing—and possibly criminal—pro, I plug it back in. "I'll see you soon." I hang up, breathing in relief when the alarm doesn't go off. But it has me questioning if I broke it. I honestly wouldn't be that surprised with how old it looks. I put it completely back together anyway then slip out of the building.

The rain is coming down so hard that visibility is limited, which might be a good thing, since it makes it less easier for someone to spot me in case Miss Metherbee returns to her store and realizes someone broke in.

My boots slash through the puddles as I sprint toward the car. Then I slide in, close the door, and start up the engine, flipping on the wiper blades. I half-expect zombie girl to appear in the passenger seat, but she doesn't.

Nothing else happens other than flashes of lighting and thunder roaring across the sky, while silence has settled around me. An unsettling silence. Like a warning that something bad is about to happen. I find myself longing for that rush I felt when I snuck into the store.

I grip the steering wheel as the revelation presses against my chest, my gaze straying to the rearview mirror. My hair is sopping wet, my makeup is a bit smeared, and my eyes look familiar yet foreign.

"Just who the hell were you, Harlynn?" I whisper to myself.

Better yet, what the hell did I used to do?

CHAPTER 11

Ten minutes later, I'm heading across the parking lot at the sheriff's office. The rain has settled to a drizzle, but the ground is flooded and my boots and the bottom half of my legs end up soaked from dirty puddles by the time I enter the building. I've been here a handful of times before and, for the most part, the place is always pretty dead. Not zombie dead, of course, but like sleepy dead. Hence how shock trickles through me as I enter and the sound of buzzing business immediately washes over me.

"What the hell?" I mutter as I peer around.

The front desk is about as empty as it normally is. Not a single person sitting in any of the chairs. Jane, though, the twenty-something-year-old secretary is frantically working to answer all the phone calls coming in at once.

Beside the front desk is where all the deputies' desks are located. Usually, a few deputies are lounging around in the area, but today, the place is crammed with uniformed men and women who are frantically rushing around or talking on the phones.

"Holy shit," I murmur. "It's like chaos swept through here or something."

"It's the murder." Kingsley steps up beside me, startling the living bejesus out of me. He looks stressed out with strands of his blond hair sticking up in all sorts of directions. "It has everyone in a panic. And, apparently, the panic is making everyone think they need to call in and see what's going on." He exhales loudly, glancing at the desk area then back at me. "I love this town and everything, but people really need to learn to stay out of stuff that doesn't concern them. I mean, what happens if there's a real emergency and all the lines are busy?"

"Well, considering it takes, like, ten minutes tops to get basically anywhere in this town, I'm assuming they'd just run down here," I offer, hoping to alleviate some of his stress.

"Yeah. Good point." He stuffs his hands into his pockets. "But that still doesn't mean I approve of all this madness." He gives a quick gesture at the desks then nods for me to follow him as he turns and heads toward the front desk. "Come on; let's go see what's going on with Miss May."

I trail after him, listening to Jane ramble, "No, we're handling it." A pause. "Yes, I understand your concern, but I can't give out any of the details about the murder." She glances up at Kingsley as he passes her desk, rolls her eyes, and mouths, "*Oh my God!*"

"Losing your mind yet, Jane?" Kingsley says with a teasing grin.

Shaking her head, she covers the receiver of the phone and whispers, "I forgot how much people around here are nosey fuckers."

He chuckles, stealing a sucker from a jar on her desk. "Yeah, they are. But what I'm wondering is how in the heck you forgot about that. Do I need to remind you of graduation night?"

She laughs, her hand still covering the phone. "Oh my God, I completely forgot about that."

"I have no idea how you could." Kingsley pops the sucker into his mouth. "It'll be branded into my mind forever."

The way she giggles makes me wonder what the hell happened on graduation night. At the same time, I'm not sure I want to know.

A sadness comes over me then. Did I have a graduation night? Do I have memories that would make people giggle? Are there people out there who I share memories with?

"Yeah, mine, too." Jane stares up at Kingsley while nibbling on her bottom lip. "I'm actually glad you brought that up, because I've been meaning to ask if maybe you want to go out sometimes after work and get a drink. Maybe talk about old times and play a game of pool or something." She flutters her eyelashes at him with hope sparkling in her eyes.

I'm not surprised she has a thing for him. Like I mentioned before, Kingsley is gorgeous and sweet. I'm kind of surprised he isn't dating someone already.

I glance between the two of them, trying to picture them together. They would look good together—Jane with her long, blonde hair and pretty, heart-shaped face, and Kingsley with his ... well, everything. But ... I don't know. For some reason, I can't conjure up an image of them holding hands and walking side by side down the road. Not that it matters.

Why am I even overanalyzing this?

I wait for Kingsley to tell her yes, but he just scratches the back of his neck and shifts his weight.

"Um ... I'm not sure what my schedule is like ... Can I check and get back to you?"

The discomfort in his tone makes even me uncomfortable. And it apparently causes Jane to talk like she just inhaled a bunch of helium, her voice rising about ten octaves as she sputters, "Oh, yeah, of course. You know what? I think I might be super busy for the next few weeks anyway. I probably should've checked my schedule before I even asked." She lets out a forced laugh. "Sometimes I can be so ditzy."

Kingsley scratches his arm. "Yeah, so can I sometimes."

Silence stretches between them, the phones ringing in the background, neither one of them looking each other in the eye. Can you say awkward?

I clear my throat, trying to draw one of them out of their uncomfortable stupors. "Um ... We should probably go see what's going on with Miss May," I remind Kingsley.

Kingsley blinks at me, a drop of relief washing over his features. "Yeah, you're right." He signals for me to follow him as he rushes away from the front desk, practically running to his office door.

I start after him, sneaking a glance in Jane's direction as I pass the front desk. She's still holding the phone in her hand, staring off into space like she's not quite sure what to do next.

I stop in front of her desk. "It'll be okay," I say, which is weird since I barely know her.

She blinks up at me. "Yeah, I know. I was just ..." She sighs heavily. "I just like him so much. I have for a very long time. And it's taken me forever to work up the courage to ask him out, so ..." Tears pool in her eyes, but she hastily sucks them back. "I don't even know why I'm surprised. Everyone knows Kingsley doesn't date."

My eyes widen. "*Really*? Like ever?"

She nods, rubbing her nose as she hangs up the phone. "Yeah, even in high school, he never had a girlfriend. Not a serious one anyway." She ignores the phones ringing, propping her elbows on the desk and lowering her head into her hands, a quiet sigh slipping from her.

I feel bad for her.

Rejection. Have I ever felt that? I think I may have since this overwhelming need to make her feel better overcomes me.

"Maybe he's never had a serious girlfriend because he doesn't want a girlfriend," I suggest.

She lifts her head to look at me with a crease between her brows. "What do you mean?"

I shrug, resting my arms on top of the desk. "Maybe he wants a boyfriend instead."

She shakes her head. "No, I don't think that's it. He may not have really dated anyone seriously, but I know for a fact that he hooked up with girls in high school."

"That doesn't necessarily mean anything."

"Yeah, I know. But I still don't think that's it. I mean, I see him check out women all the time. He's subtle about it, but it happens." She gives a short pause, mulling something over before leaning toward me and lowering her voice. "Okay, you didn't hear this from me, but you know how we were just talking about graduation night?"

I nod, eager to hear the story, which makes me question just how much this town has rubbed off on me. "Yeah."

She sneaks a glance around then leans closer. "Let's just say that it involved a dare, Kingsley, me, no clothes, and a giant pool of Jell-O. And trust me; I know for a fact that he enjoyed my naked body."

I press my lips together, uncertain how to react and kind of wishing I hadn't been curious. "Okay, maybe you're right then."

"Oh, I'm totally right," she assures me, leaning back and tapping her temple with her fingertip. "I have a sixth sense about these things."

And I have a six sense about death, but I'm not about to utter that aloud. Although, a small part of me wishes I could. Wishes I had someone I could trust to talk to about whatever is going on with me. But I don't, and I'm not sure I ever will.

"Anyway, I better get back to work." She reaches for the phone. "It was nice talking to you, Harlynn. You should come hang out with me and my friends sometime. We go bar hopping twice a month, and every other Saturday, we take turns hosting these killer mixers." She doesn't wait for me to respond as she answers the phone, so I figure she's just being polite.

It's not like I want to go to a mixer or go bar hopping in Hollows Grove, which has a total of three bars, one of which I work at. Still, a drop of loneliness does trickle through me as I walk away from the desk.

Besides working at the bar and helping Miss May, I don't have much of a social life, something I've never really thought about it until now. Now that I have, I realize how secluded my life has been. I'm not sure if that's what I really want.

Maybe if I had the answer, I could start figuring out my past. Unfortunately, one never comes to me. What does come to me, though, is a splitting headache as the sound of someone yelling suddenly pierces the room.

No, not yelling.

Screaming.

"Where is she!" Mallory, a fifty-something-year-old woman with long, black hair and who just so happens to be Douglas's wife, runs into the sheriff's office, screaming at the top of her lungs. Her face is soaked with rain, and she's severely out of breath. "Where is that murdering bitch!"

The chattering that had been filling the sheriff's office

quiets; the only background noise the relentless ringing of phones.

Jane springs to her feet and hurries around the desk. "Hey, Mallory, let's go find the deputy working your husband's case, okay?"

Mallory glares at her. "I don't want to talk to a goddamn useless deputy. What I want is to talk to the bitch who murdered my husband." Her gaze lands on me, and her nostrils flare. "You know where she is." She rushes toward me, clutching her purse. "I know you do, so tell me!" Her voice echoes throughout the building and causes me to flinch.

"I'm sorry for what happened, I really am, but Miss May didn't kill your husband, Mallory," I tell her, trying to sound as confident as possible.

"You're a liar." She gets in my face. "I can smell it all over you. You're just like her—a little liar."

"Like who?" I question.

"You know who." She pokes me in the forehead, totally throwing me off. But not as much as the abrupt drop in room temperature.

I sneak a glance around, half-expecting zombie girl to be looming in the corner, but she's not.

As I return my gaze back to Mallory, she inches toward me and lowers her voice to a whisper, the stench of her whiskey breath burning my nostrils. "You're just like her."

"Who?" I press.

I'm aware she's drunk, but sometimes people accidentally tell the truth when they're trashed.

"Miss May," she whispers, her eyes wild with mania. "You're a killer!"

Maybe if I knew who I was, I might've disregarded her statement. But I don't, so she could be right.

Am I a killer?

"Don't be stupid." Zombie girl materializes beside me.

I glare at her, wondering how she read my thoughts and also wanting to demand that she tell me who knows about paranormals, like she promised she would, but I can't talk to her in front of all these people, especially when so many are talking to me.

Two deputies appear by Mallory's side and guide her away, one of them telling her, "Come on, Mallory; let's go get you some coffee."

"I don't need any damn coffee," she slurs. "I need justice ..." Her voice fades away as the deputies steer her into an office and shut the door.

"Are you okay?" Kingsley steps up behind me and places a hand on my shoulder, startling me for the second time in ten minutes.

I didn't even hear him walk up. Then again, Mallory

was screaming in my face so loudly my ears are now ringing.

I bob my head up and down as I look at him. "Yeah, I'm fine ... I just ..." I sigh. "Why is she so convinced Miss May did this?"

"She's probably not. Mallory is just the kind of person who believes the gossip she hears. She's also always been a really angry drunk." He yanks his fingers through his hair, making the blond strands go askew. "I honestly should've known this was coming."

I rub my lips together. "Yeah, maybe." I can't help thinking of what zombie girl told me, how some people know about paranormals existing. If Kingsley is one of those people, could I tell him what I found in Beth's office?

I mentally roll my eyes at myself. Even if he did believe in paranormals, he's the sheriff and I committed a crime to get that information.

Kingsley's eyes suddenly search mine. I'm unsure what sort of expression I'm pulling, but it seems to confuse him a bit.

"Come on; let's go talk in my office, okay?" he suggests.

I nod and follow him across the front area with the lingering stench of whiskey stuck in my nose, the eerie sensation of coldness, and a feeling of being watched sending goosebumps sprouting across my flesh. The sensation is so great that I peer over my shoulder.

All that's there, though, is zombie girl. And weirdly, she looks afraid.

She's not looking at me, though, but over beside the front doors. I can't see anything there, but when my eyes stray in that direction, that cold feeling magnifies. What that means, I haven't got a clue.

Story of my goddamn life.

CHAPTER 12

"So, how are you doing with all this?" Kingsley asks as he pours me a cup of coffee.

We're in his office, and I'm sitting in a chair that's in front of his desk, looking around at the photos on his walls, the files stacked on his desk, the books on his shelf. Just being nosey, basically. Most of the books he has are crime mysteries. Although, weirdly, a few don't have titles. They look old, leather-bound, and thick.

Maybe he's into books?

I don't know a ton about Kingsley, so I'm not sure. But I really haven't tried to get to know him. I've honestly not put a lot of effort into trying to get to know anyone besides Miss May, and even she's still kind of a mystery to me. I don't think I'm a snob or anything; I've just felt so out of place since I woke up in that alley. Maybe it's time to try to put in some effort. With Miss May currently being behind bars, I've become painfully aware how lonely I'd be without her.

Maybe I'll take Jane up on her offer of going out with her and her friends. Yeah, you know what? I think I will. But after I get Miss May out of jail.

"I'm doing okay," I tell Kingsley as he turns and hands me a mug of coffee. "Well, as okay as I can be. It's frustrating me, though, knowing Miss May is in jail for a crime she didn't commit."

"I know. But we're going to get her out of here," he assures me, sitting down in the chair that's behind the desk. "I just need to look into the case more. There has to be a clue somewhere or someone who saw something that proves Miss May didn't do this."

"What evidence is there against her anyway?" I ask, setting the mug down on his desk.

He scratches his wrist, appearing a bit uncomfortable. "I can't really disclose that information, Harlynn. Not with the case still open."

"Right." For some dumbass reason, I'd almost forgotten he was the sheriff.

I lean forward, resting my arms on the desk. "Well, how do we find some evidence to prove her innocence?"

The corners of his lips tug downward. "I don't want to sound rude, but this isn't a *we* thing. This sort of stuff—

crimes and murder—it's dangerous, especially in this town. You need to be careful, okay?"

His *especially in this town* remark has me wondering ..."Why is this town any more dangerous than another town?" I question with an arch of my brow.

Does he know about this whole paranormals-existing thing?

"It's not any different," he answers a little too quickly. When I lift my brow in a questioning manner, he sighs. "Look, I just want you to be careful; that's all. I know Miss May didn't do this, which means the murderer is still out there."

"Right." I get the feeling that he's lying to me but decide not to push it. "So, what're you going to do to find some clues to prove Miss May's innocence?"

"You could always tell him about the clue you found," zombie girl whispers in my ear.

She scares me so badly that I startle, my body jolting.

"Is everything okay?" Kingsley asks, his worried gaze sweeping across me.

"Yep," I answer in way too high of a tone then quickly clear my throat. "I just really want to get Miss May out of jail. She's always been so kind to me. I just want to help her like she's helped me."

"Then you better tell him about the clue you found." Zombie girl steps up beside me, bringing the stench of rot with her, her one good eye hanging out of the socket. She reaches up and pops it back in, causing my stomach to churn.

I can't say anything to her without looking crazy, so I sneak her a *shut up* look, because she's crazy if she thinks I'm going to tell Kingsley about the clue I found, and for several different reasons, one being that I was committing a crime when I discovered it.

Kingsley's expression softens. "We'll get Miss May out of jail." He reaches across the desk and places a hand on mine. "I promise."

For the weirdest moment, I feel a connection to him, like a spark flickering inside me. But then he pulls away and the spark fizzles.

So weird.

He reclines back in the seat with his thinking face on. "I just need to find a good starting point to this mystery," he mutters more to himself. "All it usually takes is one clue, and then there should be a trail." He swivels the chair from side to side. "Maybe if I go back to the park and look around ... there might be something there that someone else hasn't seen."

"Or maybe if you told him what you found," zombie girl chimes in again. "Stop being such a scaredy cat."

I just shake my head. I may be clueless sometimes, but

that doesn't mean I'm just going to confess to a crime I committed only an hour ago.

"He knows, Harlynn," zombie girl says with an annoyed sigh.

I look at her confusedly, like *huh?*

"Kingsley knows that paranormals exist in the world. I told you some people know, and he's one of them." She gives a pressing glance at the bookshelf. "Those books down there that don't have titles contain information and legends about all sorts of creatures. They were given to him by his father. And his father got them from his father. And so on and so on."

I silently gape at her. Is she being serious? Or messing with me? It's really hard to tell sometimes.

She smirks. "There. Now I don't owe you anything anymore." With that, she evaporates into thin air, leaving me to figure out the rest on my own.

I'm left faced with two choices: keep what I know to myself and try to solve this mystery by myself, which could lead to Miss May staying in jail for a very long time. Or I can tell Kingsley what I found and hope that it's enough to lead him to the truth about Douglas's murder. Of course, I'll get put in jail for breaking and entering, but Miss May could be released from jail, so ...

I internally sigh. Well, I guess I just discovered another trait about myself.

"I need to tell you something." I dig out my phone. "Or, well, show you something." I tap open the photo I took while I was in Miss Metherbee's store then slide my phone across the desk.

A pucker forms between his brows as he picks up my phone. Then, once he sees the photo, the confusion erases.

He glances up at me. "Where did you find this?" Suspicion fills his eyes.

I nervously pick at my fingernails. "Um ... In Miss Metherbee's store. It was on the back of a receipt from a purchase Douglas made from her. A purchase that totaled ten thousand dollars. But I don't know what it was for since the item was blacked out by marker."

He studies me, his gaze burrowing into me. "How did you get into Miss Metherbee's store?"

Aw, crap. I really was hoping he'd be so distracted by what I found that he'd forget to ask that.

I lift a shoulder, giving a casual shrug. "Would you believe me if I said the door was wide open?"

He cocks a brow. "Harlynn—"

"Oh, fine." I grimace, slumping back in the seat. "I broke in to look for clues and found that."

"You broke in to her store?" he repeats with a frown.

I nod. "Yep. And, since I'm being so truthful right

now, I should probably tell you that I disarmed the security alarm to get in."

He stares at me like I'm crazy. "You do realize I'm the sheriff, right?"

"Really?" I thrum my finger against my lips. "Huh. I always thought you just liked wearing uniforms," I try to tease, but he doesn't even so much as blink.

Awesome, Harlynn. Way to make this worse.

I guess it's behind bars for me.

He assesses me so closely that I almost start to squirm. "Why did you even look in Miss Metherbee's store to begin with?"

"Because I had a hunch." Which is the partial truth. I'm not about to tell him the entire truth, though—that I can see zombies. Sure, zombie girl said I could trust Kingsley with the receipt thing, but I'm not about to confess how weird I am. No, that's a secret I'm going to take to the grave. No pun intended.

"You had a hunch?" he repeats my words, and I can tell he doesn't quite believe me. Then he straightens in his chair and leans forward, assessing me. "How much do you know?"

I stare at him, wondering if zombie girl was telling the truth about him.

"How much do *you* know?" I counter.

He drums his fingers against the desk, his gaze fixed on me. "I meant about Hollows Grove."

"Um, about three months' worth," I reply, lifting a shoulder. "Which is really all I know about anything."

"You sure about that?" he questions with a cock of his brow.

I frown. "Wait ... Do you think I'm lying about not being able to remember who I am?" I'm not sure if I should be offended or not, but I kind of am.

He thinks I'm a liar?

Well, I guess I kind of am, but not about that.

And I'm not really sure why him not believing me hurts me a bit, but it does.

"I don't know. Are you?" he questions. "Maybe you can remember who you are and just came here to hide from something."

Wow, that one really hurt.

"Is that what you really think of me?" I guess I can't really blame him. It is weird how I showed up here without being able to remember anything. Still, I suddenly don't feel as comfortable around him. I think I need to leave.

I start to stand up when he springs to his feet. I tense, worried he's about to arrest me for breaking and entering, and maybe because he thinks I've been lying about everything.

Could I even get arrested for something like that?

"Harlynn, wait," he says quickly. "I'm sorry. I don't know why I went off on you like that. I just ..." He blows out a heavy sigh. "I think I picked up some bad habits from my father, despite how much I tried not to."

I turn to face him, eyeing him over. "Does that mean you believe me that I can't remember anything before I showed up here? Because I wasn't lying about that."

He nods. "I believe you. I always have. I just got a little carried away there for a moment because of that photo you showed me."

"Oh." I pause, trying to decide if I still trust him. Weirdly, I feel like I do. "Does that mean you know what that symbol means?"

Searching my eyes again, he says, "I recognize it. Do you?"

I shake my head. "No."

He silently stares at me for a moment. "How much do you know about this town?"

This is the second time he asked me this, and I have a feeling it has to do with what zombie girl told me about paranormals existing. And now I have to make the choice: either I can pretend I know nothing about the strange stuff that goes bump in the night or confide in him that I'm aware weird things exist in this world that some people can't see.

"I know some stuff about this town. Like ... things that might not seem real ..." I bite my tongue, chickening out.

Yep, apparently, I was a chicken in another life.

Well, not literally of course.

Kingsley must fill in the blanks, because he says, "You know paranormals exist, don't you?"

Well, there you go. Apparently, Kingsley isn't a chicken.

Pressing my lips together, I nod. "Yeah, I do."

It's like a mask has been removed from his face. That's how much stress leaves his expression. "Thank God. I thought I was going to have to pretend my way through all this."

"All what?" I ask as he walks over to the bookshelf and grabs one of those thick, leather-bound, untitled books.

He stands up and turns toward me. "Usually, when I have to work cases like this—magic related cases"—he sets the book down on the desk and starts fanning through the pages—"and I'm not around people who are aware that magic exists, I have to make up stories. It can get really fucking tiring."

Well, okay then, I guess we're going to just jump right into this.

"I imagine it would get tiring." In fact, I know this firsthand, seeing as how I've spent three months pretending like a rotting dead girl isn't following me around, whispering snarky comments into my ear.

I step over beside Kingsley to see what's on the pages, but they're blank.

What the crap?

"Do you mind if I ask how you know about this?" he asks as he continues flipping through blank pages.

"I honestly don't know how I know." I sit down on the edge of his desk. "I wasn't lying about not being able to remember anything before I woke up in that alley. But I do know that I've seen some things that are"—I waver for the right word—"weird."

He glances up at me, intrigue sparkling in his eyes. "What sort of things?"

While we're being pretty open at the moment, I don't want to tell him about how I can see zombies. I'm not sure why. It's just a feeling in my gut.

"I saw a zombie once," I offer the partial truth.

"Really?" He seems intrigued by that. "I didn't realize those existed."

"Oh." Crap, I should've said something else, like a vampire or something.

Luckily, he doesn't press me for more details, returning his attention back to the book.

"I honestly don't know much about this," I continue on. "You seem to, though."

"I do," he replies distractedly. "I've known my whole life, basically."

I open my mouth, about to ask him if he can explain some things to me. Maybe if I knew more about magic and paranormals, I could figure out why in the hell I can see zombies. And maybe that could lead me to figuring out more about who I am. But before I can say anything, he stops on a page and says, "There we go."

I lean over to look at the page then frown. "Um ... You do realize that's a blank page, right?"

The corners of his lips lift into a small smirk. "To a normal person, yeah. But I was born with the ability of sight. That's part of the reason why my family knows paranormals exist."

"What's sight?" I ask.

He rubs his lips together as if deciding if he wants to tell me. "It's basically the ability to see all things that are magical." He glances down at the page. "Some people think it's a curse."

"Do you think it is?"

"Sometimes." He doesn't elaborate, picking up my phone that's still on the desk and looking at the photo again. Then he looks back at the page. Then the photo. Back and forth. And back and forth. "There we go." He shuts the book, hands me back my phone, and then puts the book back on the shelf without saying anything else.

"There we go what?" I ask, stuffing my phone into my pocket as he moves back behind his desk and picks up the phone.

"I know what that symbol is," he informs me as he dials a number. "And I know who killed Mr. Douglas."

"Okay ..." I wait for him to tell me, but he just stares off into space with the phone pressed to his ear. Finally, I can't take the suspense anymore. "Come on, Kingsley; tell me who killed him."

He blinks at me like he totally forgot I was standing there. "He actually did it himself."

I slant back in surprise. That's so not what I thought he was going to say. "What does that mean?"

"Yeah, I'll hold," he says into the phone then looks back at me. "That symbol that was on the back of the receipt is linked to a ritual someone can perform if they want to turn into a vampire without having to be bit by one. In order to perform the ritual, you need a device called a *portal vitisque repertory*. Or, basically, a portal finder. And I'm guessing that blacked out item on the receipt was for one, since Miss Metherbee has a reputation for selling magical, black market devices."

Is he freaking kidding me? After she accused *me* of selling tables and chairs on the black market?

"I know it's a lot to take in," he tells me, reaching out

and giving my hand a squeeze. "But I promise this is a good thing, because it proves Miss May is innocent."

Again, his touch causes my skin to spark.

"Does that mean that the deputies around here believe in that sort of stuff, too?"

He shakes his head, withdrawing his hand from mine and causing the sparks to fizzle. "Not all of them, but enough."

"Oh." I frown. "Does Miss May?"

"No, she doesn't. At least, not that I'm aware of." He pauses. "Well, unless you've told her?"

"No. I honestly thought I was just crazy."

He cracks a smile. "You're far from crazy, Har."

Something about the way he says it and the way he's smiling at me causes that spark to flicker inside me again.

I'm about to ask him if he feels it, too, like maybe it's some sort of magical thing, but whoever he's waiting for on the phone decides to answer his call at that precise moment.

"Hey," he says into the receiver while holding up a finger in my direction and mouthing, *"Hold on,"* to me. "Yeah, I need you to prepare for Miss May's release." He pauses. "Because I have evidence that proves her innocence." Another pause. "No, Douglas did it to himself ... Well, we'll have to look into it more, but I'm pretty sure he turned himself into a vampire." He remains silent for a moment or two. "Just hurry up and call the morgue. I promise you the body won't be there."

He blows out a sigh then looks at me. "You doing okay? You look a bit pale?"

I nod, even though I'm not sure if I am. In fact, I kind of feel woozy. But it's been an overwhelming day.

He suddenly frowns and his lips part, but then he returns his attention back to the phone. "Of course I was right," he says into the phone. "Okay, see you in a few." He hangs up then looks at me.

"They're preparing for Miss May's release. That should only take about an hour."

A wave of relief washes over me. "Thank God."

"Don't get too relaxed just yet. This means Douglas is still running around town, which means a vampire is running loose around town."

That sends a shiver down my spine. "Do vampires kill people?"

He seems mildly amused by my question. "Sometimes. But I'll find Douglas before he can get that far. I have excellent vampire tracking skills."

He crosses the room, places his hand on the small of my back, and ushers me toward the door. "When Miss May is released, I want you to go straight home and lock the doors, okay? I'll let you know when I catch Douglas."

I nod as he pulls the door open.

"I just have one more question, though." Well, I have a ton of questions, but now doesn't seem like the time to ask him since he's in a hurry.

He pauses with his hand still resting on the small of my back. "Okay."

I twist to face him, and his hand ends up resting on my hip. "What's the point of turning into a vampire and faking your own death? Plus, why set Miss May up? At least, that's why I'm assuming Beth told you it was Miss May."

His lips curve into a frown. "How did you find that out?"

I shrug. "I had another hunch."

He meticulously studies me with his pretty gaze. "You seem to have a lot of hunches."

"Yeah," I say, acting as blasé as I can.

He rubs his lips together as he picks up a pencil and starts drumming it against the desk. "To answer your first question, more than likely, Douglas wanted the immortality and eternal youth that comes with vampirism. Although, he was older, so the youth part doesn't really apply here," he says with a crinkle at his brow. "I have a feeling Douglas might be trying to hide from something."

I'm a little surprised he let my whole I had a hunch comment slide so easily, but maybe he believed me.

Doubtful, though. No, I have a feeling he's avoiding the subject for some reason.

"Why do you think that?"

"Just a hunch." He gives me a little smirk.

I bite back a smile. "Touché."

He smiles at me as he opens the door and steers me out of the office. But the moment we step out, his smile fizzles, a serious expression taking over his face.

I want to ask him so many more questions, since he seems so knowledgeable about all of this stuff, but I can tell he's in a hurry to get this taken care of, so I keep the questions to myself. For now anyway.

He must sense my need to know more, though, because he says, "After this is all taken care of, maybe in a few days, you and I can go out and talk about this more, because I can tell you have a lot of questions."

"A ton," I admit. "And yeah, let's do that. Thanks."

We just happen to be passing Jane's desk at that very moment, and she starts to smile at us when her gaze drops to where Kingsley's hand is back to resting on my lower back. Then she instantly frowns.

I want to walk over there and tell her that it doesn't mean anything, that Kingsley is basically just pushing me out of his office so he can go chase down a vampire, but I'm not sure if Jane knows about paranormals. Plus, Kingsley doesn't give me a chance, quickly guiding me past the desk until we reach the front waiting area. Only then does he lower his hand from my back.

"Are you going to be okay waiting here for Miss May by yourself?" he asks, reaching into his pocket.

"Yeah, I'll be fine," I tell him then whisper, "Go slay a vampire or whatever."

He presses back a smile, seeming amused. "All right." He starts to leave then turns around. "Be careful, okay? And call me if you need anything."

I nod, and then he walks away, the conversation ending. But it's definitely not over yet. We have a lot more to talk about.

A lot, lot more.

CHAPTER 13

I wait around for Miss May for about an hour before a deputy brings her out from the back. I wonder if he knows about paranormals, too, or if he's just following orders.

"Hey," I tell Miss May, so damn happy to see her.

"Hi, hon," she replies, looking tired and annoyed, glaring at the deputy as he drops her off.

"You can go now," she tells him. "And don't bother asking me to bake cookies for your mom this year, because the answer is hell no!"

The deputy sighs and walks away, heading toward the desk area.

"Who was that?" I ask Miss May as we push through the doors and step outside.

"He's the son of one of the women in my book club,"

she explains as we start down the sidewalk, heading for the car. "I usually bake her cookies every year for her birthday, but not anymore! I've done so much shit for this town, and they all repay me by arresting me! This is bullshit!"

I've never seen her so upset before. Then again, I've only known her for three months. Her anger, though, is completely justified.

"From now on, everyone should start baking *you* cookies," I tell her, digging the car keys out of my pocket.

She cracks a smile at that. "Damn straight."

We exchange a smile then climb into the car.

It's a quiet drive, Miss May stuck in her own thoughts and me in mine. I keep thinking about Kingsley out there, chasing around a vampire with a stake in his hand. I'm not sure if that's how it works. I'm not sure about anything. I just hope that I'll learn more about this whole paranormal world thing when Kingsley and I go out in a few days.

By the time we arrive home, it's dark and Miss May hasn't said a word since we got into the car. I'm starting to get a little worried.

"Are you okay?" I ask as I park the car in the driveway.

She nods, blinking from her daze and looking at me. "Yeah. Sorry, hon. I'm just thinking about what happened today."

"Was jail awful?" I ask as I shut off the engine and

headlights, leaving the only light coming from the neighbors' porch lights.

She shakes her head. "Not really. I was the only one in there, and I know all the deputies. It just frustrates me that they arrested me to begin with." She pushes the door open to get out. "And until they solve the case, the people in this town are going to gossip about me."

I suddenly realize Kingsley never explained what he was going to tell the town about what happened to Douglas. What will the story be?

Sighing, Miss May climbs out of the car, drawing me from my thoughts.

I hop out, too, then shut the door and meet her around the front of the car. "I'm sorry this happened to you," I tell her, pocketing the keys.

She offers me a tired smile. "It's not your fault, Harlynn." She pats my arm. "How about we go inside and have some tea and cookies? I think that might cheer me up a bit."

I smile. "That sounds nice. Can I just run up to my room really quickly, though? My clothes got drenched in the rainstorm today, and I'd really like to change."

"Of course. I honestly want to take a quick shower, too, and wash this day off me. Meet you in the kitchen in half an hour?"

I nod, and then we start to part ways, me heading

toward the room above the garage and her toward the house. But right as I reach the bottom of the stairway, I pause and turn around.

"Miss May?" I call out.

She pauses from unlocking the door and twists around to look at me. "Yeah?"

"Make sure to lock the door until I get there, okay? With what happened today, I just want to make sure you're safe."

"I will," she assures. "And the same goes for you."

I nod then start up the stairs, taking my time to make sure she gets inside safely. The moment she does, I haul ass up the stairs, wanting to get the hell out of the darkness and into my house.

I quickly unlock the door, my heart racing as I envision Douglas out there, creeping around in the dark. So, by the time I get inside, I'm a mess of anxiety, only calming down once I get the door locked. Then I flip on the light and start to remove my shirt to take a shower, but freeze, my eyes widening in horror.

My room has been trashed, all my belongings have been thrown around, and the furniture has been tipped over. Even the couch cushions have been ripped open. It's as if someone was searching for something. And worse, painted on the wall in what I'm hoping is red paint are the words: *I know what you are.*

"What the fuck?" I breathe out, my heart pounding in my chest.

I'd worry someone was still here, but since the room is a loft and I can see every inch of the place from where I'm standing, I know I'm alone.

Zombie girl appears by my side.

Okay, maybe not totally alone.

She doesn't look even a bit shocked as she peers around the trashed room. "You've been found, and that's not a good thing."

"Why not?" I glance at her. "And found by whom?"

She doesn't answer, leaving me to wonder what she knows. Mostly, I just wonder who knows about me and what they know.

"I guess we're going to start working on another case," zombie girl suddenly states.

I gape at her. "What?"

She gestures at the wall. "We need to figure out who did this, right?"

I nod. "I guess so."

She smiles, which looks all sorts of weird since she doesn't have any teeth. "So, we're starting another case."

"When did we ever work on a case?"

She looks at me like I'm an idiot. "Today, with Miss May."

"We didn't solve that," I inform her. "Kingsley did."

She rolls her eye. "Don't give him all the credit. He only solved it because of the photo you gave him. You know, the one you took after you used those awesome skills of yours to break into Miss Metherbee's store."

Maybe she's a little bit right, but ... "I'm not a detective."

"How do you know that for sure? You don't even know who you are."

She's right again, but ..."Well, someone else clearly does know who I am." I gesture at the wall.

"And if you figure out who that someone is, you may be able to find out more about yourself," she says enticingly.

Again, she's right. Still ... "Just because I can break into a store doesn't mean I'm a detective. However, I want to figure out who did this and what they know about me."

"Good," she says then grows serious. "Just be careful. There's a reason why you woke up in an alley with no memory of who you are." With that, she poofs herself away, leaving me to wonder what she knows about me.

Leaving me to wonder a lot of things.

What I do know is that she's ... right. I need to figure out who painted this on my wall. And then I need to find out what they know about me.

Because that might be the key to figuring out my past.

To figuring out who the hell I am.

ABOUT THE AUTHOR

Jessica Sorensen is a *New York Times* and *USA Today* bestselling author who lives in the snowy mountains of Wyoming. When she's not writing, she spends her time reading and hanging out with her family.

For information: jessicasorensen.com

ALSO BY JESSICA SORENSEN

Harlynn's Mystery Investigations:

Sugar Cookies & Zombie Secrets

Untitled (releasing early 2020)

Monster Academy for the Magical Series:

Monster Academy for the Magical

Monster Academy for the Magical: The Deadly Four

Untitled (coming soon)

The Secret Series:

The Prelude of Ella and Micha

The Secret of Ella and Micha

The Forever of Ella and Micha

The Temptation of Lila and Ethan

The Ever After of Ella and Micha

The Secret Mysteries of Star Grove: The Road Trip Interrupted
(coming soon)

Other Secret Series books:

The Prelude of Ella and Micha

Lila and Ethan: Forever and Always

Ella and Micha: Infinitely and Always

Enchanted Chaos Series:

Enchanted Chaos

Shimmering Chaos

Iridescent Chaos

Entangled Chaos (coming soon)

Capturing Magic:

Chasing Wishes

Chasing Magic

Untitled (coming soon)

Chasing Hadley Harlyton:

Chasing Hadley

Falling for Hadley

Holding onto Hadley

Untitled (coming soon)

Cursed Hadley:

Cursed Hadley

Enchanting Hadley (coming soon)

<u>**Tangled Realms:**</u>

Forever Violet

Untitled (coming soon)

<u>**Curse of the Vampire Queen:**</u>

Tempting Raven

Enchanting Raven

Alluring Raven

Untitled (coming soon)

<u>**Unraveling You Series:**</u>

Unraveling You

Raveling You

Awakening You

Inspiring You

Every Single Breath

Untitled (coming soon)

<u>**Unexpected Series:**</u>

The Unexpected Complications of Revenge

Untitled (coming soon)

<u>**Shadow Cove Series:**</u>

What Lies in the Darkness

What Lies in the Dark

Untitled (coming soon)

Mystic Willow Bay Series:

The Secret Life of a Witch

Broken Magic

Untitled (coming soon)

Standalones:

The Forgotten Girl

The Honeyton Series:

The Illusion of Annabella

Untitled (coming soon)

Rebels & Misfits Series:

Confessions of a Kleptomaniac

Rules of a Rebel and a Shy Girl

Secrets We Buried

Untitled (coming soon)

The Fareland Society:

Opposite of Ordinary

Untitled (coming soon)

<u>Broken City Series:</u>

Nameless

Forsaken

Oblivion

Forbidden (coming soon)

<u>Guardian Academy Series:</u>

Entranced

Entangled

Enchanted

The Forest of Shadow & Bone

Entice

Charmed

Untitled (coming soon)

<u>Sunnyvale Series:</u>

The Year I Became Isabella Anders

The Year of Falling in Love

The Year of Second Chances

The Year of Kia and Isa

Untitled (coming soon)

<u>**The Coincidence Series:**</u>

The Coincidence of Callie and Kayden

The Redemption of Callie and Kayden

The Destiny of Violet and Luke

The Probability of Violet and Luke

The Certainty of Violet and Luke

The Resolution of Callie and Kayden

Seth & Greyson

The Evermore of Callie & Kayden (coming soon)

<u>**The Shattered Promises Series:**</u>

Shattered Promises

Fractured Souls

Unbroken

Broken Visions

Scattered Ashes

<u>**Breaking Nova Series:**</u>

Breaking Nova

Saving Quinton

Delilah: The Making of Red

Nova and Quinton: No Regrets

Tristan: Finding Hope

Wreck Me

Ruin Me

The Fallen Star Series:

The Fallen Star

The Underworld

The Vision

The Promise

The Lost Soul

The Evanescence

The Mist of Starts (coming soon)

The Darkness Falls Series:

Darkness Falls

Darkness Breaks

Darkness Fades

The Death Collectors Series (NA and YA):

Ember X and Ember

Cinder X and Cinder

Spark X and Spark

Unbeautiful Series:

Unbeautiful

Untamed

www.ingramcontent.com/pod-product-compliance
Lightning Source LLC
Chambersburg PA
CBHW030645190726
48286CB00008B/2665